Carnival
An imprint of the Children's Division
of the Collins Publishing Group
8 Grafton Street, London W1X 3LA

Published by Carnival 1989

Copyright © East End Films 1989

ISBN 0 00 194377 4

Art Assistant Lisa Kingston

Printed and bound in Great Britain by
PURNELL BOOK PRODUCTION LIMITED
A MEMBER OF BPCC plc

Fire on the Farm

Written and illustrated by
Peter Kingston

Horace Hayseeder, the farmer, was very busy.

All morning he had been taking big bales of hay from the fields to his farmyard and was now on his way back to store them in the huge haybarn.

He was hurrying as best he could as it was nearly lunchtime and he was feeling rather hungry.

At the haybarn, Horace picked up each heavy bale and piled them one on top of the other. He had nearly finished, when he noticed the time.

"I think I'll have me lunch first," he said, "and then I'll finish off afterwards."

He sat down on the haybales, opened his sandwiches and had a nice, hot cup of tea from his flask.

When he'd finished, he leaned back and yawned, "I think I'll just have a little snooze before I start again."

And with that, he settled down amongst the haybales and was soon snoring loudly.

But while Horace was fast asleep, he missed seeing the stranger walking his dog. The silly man just couldn't have been thinking!

He took a cigarette out of his mouth and threw it over the fence!

Without a thought, the man carried on walking and whistling happily.

The cigarette landed in amongst the dry hay and it wasn't long before a thin wisp of smoke appeared only to be followed by little flames!

The little flames got bigger and bigger and soon started spreading along the bales of hay!

Meanwhile, on the other side of the barn, Horace woke up, completely unaware of the fire.

He stretched his arms, climbed back on his tractor and drove off.

But he didn't get very far. Dennis Letterleaver, the postman, ran into the

road, waving his arms and jumping up and down.

"Stop, Horace! Stop!" he yelled. "Your haybarn's on fire!"

Horace looked horrified. "Oh no!" he cried. "Jump on me tractor, Dennis, and we'll go and have a look."

But the fire was getting very fierce, flames crackling and thick, nasty smoke everywhere.

Dennis took off his postbag and started beating the flames. "I'll try and put it out with my bag, Horace," he yelled. "But you'd better get the fire brigade just in case."

Horace jumped back on his tractor and roared into the village to tell P.C. Crooknabber.

It wasn't long before everybody had heard about the fire.

Horace dashed into the little police station. "It's me haybarn, P.C. Crooknabber," he cried, pointing and waving. "Me haybarn's ablaze!"

P.C. Crooknabber looked up from his desk. "Now calm down, Horace," he said. "I'll phone the fire brigade right away."

But when he had put the phone down, he looked a bit concerned. "I'm afraid it will take them a while to get here from the Big Town," he said. "So let's go and see what we can do."

But when P.C. Crooknabber and Horace arrived at the haybarn, they saw to their horror that the fire was getting worse and worse!

"Oh dear me," sighed P.C. Crooknabber. "This is really quite serious." Horace tugged hard on P.C. Crooknabber's jacket.

"Oh no!" he cried. "Just look at the flames. They're spreading to me farmhouse now!"

What were they going to do?

By this time, everybody from the village had come to see the fire, and luckily, Percy Pennywise, the general storekeeper, had a good idea. He told the Twin Breadsnappers to run to his shop in the village and collect as many plastic buckets as they could carry.

They were soon back with armfuls of coloured buckets.

"Well done, boys," laughed Percy. "Now take them all to the river bank."

One of the twins dipped the first bucket
into the river and scooped out the water;
the other twin then passed it to P.C.
Crooknabber.

"That's it, boys," said P.C.
Crooknabber. "Keep 'em coming and
mind you don't spill any water."

It wasn't long before there were rows of buckets, brimming with water, all ready for the next stage of Percy's plan.

P.C. Crooknabber quickly arranged the villagers in a long line from the river bank all the way to the burning haybarn.

P.C. Crooknabber then took two buckets full of water and passed the first to Father Away, the priest, who passed it to Ethel Doughkneader, the baker, who

passed it to Ted Dripping, the butcher, and so on all the way to Dennis Letterleaver at the fire itself.

Bucket after bucket went along the line.

At the other end, Dennis took each bucket and threw the water onto the fire and passed the empties back.

After a little while, the flames got smaller and smaller.

"That's it!" yelled Dennis in excitement. "The fire's nearly out!"

At that moment, they all heard a siren in the distance.

"Well, I be blowed," laughed Horace. "Here comes the fire engine."

The little red engine bounced its way to the barn and screeched to a halt.

The fireman dashed up to Horace, clutching his firehose. "Er, hello!" he said, looking puzzled. "Where's the fire then?"

Horace laughed. "Well, thanks to all me friends here, especially Percy Pennywise

and his shop full of buckets, we've managed to save me farm from burning down," he said.

The firemen were very impressed with everybody in Wimpole Village, and while they sprayed the smouldering barn to make sure it was well and truly out, Horace had a great idea.

"Come on, everybody," he laughed. "All over to my house and I'll treat you all to a very special tea."

And what a special tea they had — jellies, cakes, sandwiches, lemonade.

Everybody was very happy, all except . . .

. . . the silly man who threw the cigarette away in the first place! He had watched everything from a distance, but had been too ashamed to help. He crept quietly off home with his little dog, having learnt a very big lesson.

He'll certainly remember the country code from now on.